GW00758666

Möbius Strips
and Other Stories

2/22/21

MÖBIUS STRIPS AND OTHER STORIES

love [signature]

Tom DeMarchi

Dear Rita & Sergio,

Thank you for being such a good, true friend to my mother all these years.

Rain Chain Press

Thank you, too, for checking out my book. Please feel free to stop reading when things get boring.

Love, Tom

These stories previously appeared in:
• "Mobius Strips." *Flash! Writing the Very Short Story.* Norton & Norton, 2018. (Originally published in *Quick Fiction*, issue 14, Fall 2008.)
• "Milk of Magnesia." *Flash! Writing the Very Short Story.* Norton & Norton, 2018.
• "Inside Aisles." *Cheap Pop.* (http://www.cheappoplit.com/home/2013/12/17/inside-aisles-tom-demarchi) March 18, 2014.
• "Touch That and the Doll Gets It," previously published as "Fog." *Belletrist Coterie.* Issue 1, Spring 2012.
• "Birdman." *The Pinch.* Vol. 29.2, Spring 2009.
• "Ruby, My Dear" (shorter version). *Street Weekly/Miami Herald.* July 2004.
• "Evolution." *Em.* 2001.
• "Stealing Home." *Miami Herald.* 1996.

Book design: James Barrett-Morison
Cover design: Kevin Toler

10 9 8 7 6 5 4 3 2 1

For Charlie DeMarchi

Contents

Möbius Strips

The doors are bolted, the windows sealed—of this I'm sure, just as I'm sure that Rosemary's lying beside me, beneath an itchy afghan in a bed I've slept in since I was eleven years old, a bed I had shipped via train from Peabody to Fresno to Miami, back to Peabody, back to my parents' aluminum-insulated ranch that's currently getting pelted with snow. Rosemary's jugular pulses in the red glow of my digital clock, and I wonder if the whistle I hear is wind blowing through a crack in the window, air being inhaled through her nostrils, the B&M railroad chugging past the reservoir three blocks away, or if I'm dreaming of the past, of July 1979, when Mark X—what was his last name?—and I hiked home after swimming in the reservoir and lined the tracks with pennies, watched the 2:19 whizz past, blow-dry our hair, spit copper tears at our feet.

My father shuffles down the hallway to the front door. I picture him twisting the knob, unlocking and locking the dead bolt, traipsing from window to window, unlatching and latching.

He stops in the dining room, presses his palms and forehead to the window, stares at the plowed snow barricading his driveway. He sighs at the thought of shoveling in a few hours when his stomach will churn coffee and Cheerios. A shiver sends him back down the hall to my bedroom door, where he pauses.

My mother, a nurse, says the human brain is a series of Möbius strips lined with locked filing cabinets, that neural atrophy causes us to begin losing keys at age twenty-three. My mother says crossword puzzles, a steady diet of blueberries, long walks, needlepoint, and thick history books keep those keys jingling on our hips, keep the hallways lit. My mother posits this theory weekly, as if it just occurred to her.

I wonder if my father's standing in the hallway because he's wondering if he locked the front door. Names of old golfing buddies, where he put his glasses, his age: just some of the things my father chases down dark hallways. I wonder if he wonders if he's showing signs of Alzheimer's, like Mr. Otto, a neighbor once arrested for pissing against the wall of the 7-Eleven, and who, like my father just last week, reported his car stolen after he'd forgotten where he parked.

I wonder whether I'll remember this moment: Rosemary's pulsing jugular, B&M's fading whistle, my father frozen in the hallway, cold fingertips pressing his forehead, and me—now—disentangling myself from the afghan's itchy embrace, easing into my slippers, opening my bedroom door, startling my father into saying "Jesus!," planting my index finger on his lips, taking his hand, leading him from window to window, door to door, jiggling doorknobs and testing locks, securing the house so both of us can sleep without any regard for the snow piling up outside.

Milk of Magnesia

As soon as Steve limps out of CVS, the nagging regret he'd felt just moments earlier while shoving a bottle of Milk of Magnesia down his pants for Paul, Anna's constipated father, disappears, and not only because he thinks he eluded the security guard's steely gaze, but also because he sees Anna sitting in her Mercury, parked right where they'd planned—next to the Wachovia ATM on the far side of TJ Maxx—and her pink-streaked blonde hair gives Steve's heart a little jolt of electricity. Before getting laid off from his job in the Coca-Cola warehouse thirteen months ago, Steve'd never stolen anything in his life, but what with the unemployment checks running out and Steve swallowing his pride and agreeing to move in with Paul, and then Paul getting bound up from a gastroenterological collision of diverticulitis and too much of the food bank's government-issue cheese, and Anna being six months pregnant (a boy, yet unnamed) and having her hours cut at Shear Joy Hair Salon, well, he'd had to make some compromises in the ethics department, and that was both okay and not okay with Steve, depending on his mood, and depending on how full his stomach was and how much he thought about the cells dividing in Anna's womb and how those cells were forming a son whose overall health and well-being would, sooner rather than later, depend on Steve's ability to provide a suitable and abundant environment conducive to raising a family.

CVS's doors whoosh open behind him, and before Steve makes it to Anna's car he hears a deep voice say, "You wanna show me what you got in those pants, sir? Don't even think of running 'cause I was the state champ in the

100-yard dash back in high school, and you best believe my feet've still got wings."

Even if he hadn't slipped and twisted his ankle in the bathtub last week and he'd sprinted safely to the car, Steve knows a license plate can't outrun anyone's pen.

For a moment Steve weighs his options—run or stay— neither of which can lead to anything good, so he turns and notices two things about the security guard: his nametag says "Xavier," and Xavier's wearing a wedding ring, and this reminds Steve of his own ring that he hocked two months ago to buy the Mercury a new timing belt.

"Guard" is an odd title for Xavier's job, since he doesn't guard things; on a good day he might intimidate kids from pocketing gum. He stands in plain sight to remind would-be criminals that there's an order to things, and so his presence is at best an appeal to our better angels and at base a threat of consequences, yet Xavier's hangdog expression betrays the weight of his own compromises. Instead of running, Steve wonders about Xavier's abandoned ambitions—did he one day dream of being a lawyer or a cop?—and he remembers that in fifth grade, for that hunchbacked nun, Sister Lorraine, he'd written an essay about wanting to be a cop himself.

Just then Steve notices Xavier's hand resting on the can of Mace.

"Keep calm, Xavier," he says.

"Look here, sir," Xavier says, "I know you got more than a dick in your pants. Me and you, we gotta go inside and straighten things out."

Never before had Steve's mouth been so dry; it feels as if his tongue has fallen asleep on the beach. Over his shoulder, he hears the Mercury's rattling tailpipe. "Please," he says, "this isn't who I am."

Quite against his better judgment, Steve backs toward the edge of the curb, where he senses the car has pulled up and parked, and without taking his eyes off Xavier, he reaches back and feels the passenger door handle; he raises it and pulls the door open, slides inside, and closes it—all the while keeping his eyes locked with Xavier's. Right then, as Anna starts to inch the Mercury forward, Xavier extends his hands flat, a gesture Steve decides is a wave goodbye rather than a command to halt. Something about the flattened palms and the lumbering gait tells Steve that Xavier is granting him a reprieve, and so Steve feels obligated to point to Anna's protruding belly as if to say, "I am bigger than this moment."

The image of Xavier recedes in the side-view mirror, and Steve chokes back the bile rising in his throat.

Until this moment, Steve has kept the Milk of Magnesia jocked; he looks at Anna, who smiles sadly while he unzips his fly, uncaps the bottle, takes a swig, and thinks about the near and distant future:

Very soon, they'll be back in the apartment, and Paul will gulp down the Milk of Magnesia without saying thanks or asking where they'd gotten the money to buy it, and Steve will wonder whether Xavier will have to explain himself to his boss, whether he'll lose his job, and whether he'll go home and tell his wife about the most pathetic shoplifter ever to enter the store.

Will Xavier remember this day with regret or pride? Xavier might forget the incident altogether, but Steve knows he'll remember for the rest of his life.

Years from now, when he's a father and today is nothing more than one peak in a range of shames, Steve hopes he'll have forgiven himself and has the capacity to extend his son the mercy all children require.

Zipping up his fly, Steve decides that one day he'll make Xavier proud.

Inside Aisles

I want Henry to mean it when he says we'll stay in touch. "We're friends no matter what," he says before pulling away in the U-Haul. What does "We'll stay in touch" mean? Birthday cards? Facebook pokes? And what does "You gotta give the next guy a chance" mean? What next guy? A chance to what? Fuck my mother till he's bored? When the U-Haul turns onto Hollywood Blvd., I go in the back yard and cry behind the shed until Mr. Gira leans over the fence, points his garden hose at me and asks what the hell I'm doing blubbering like a baby. "You're, what, thirteen? Be a man."

I go into the house and say, "What a tool," meaning Mr. Gira but knowing Mom'll think I mean Henry.

She's still staring into the open fridge. It's been over an hour and I wonder if I should call Grandma for help. She says, "We're never eating another soy burger."

"Or kale," I say.

"Bitter weed," she says. She opens the crisper, pulls out two heads of broccoli, hip-checks the door shut. She opens the freezer and grabs the package of soy burgers. She stomps on the trashcan pedal and dumps everything in. "Who feels like tacos?"

Henry would say that most people subsist on poison and don't even know it. He cautioned against putting the wrong things in your body, that there's only so much abuse your system can take. He'd say, "I bet you can't pronounce half the ingredients in a Twinkie. Don't put anything in your body you can't say." He'd say, "Healthy food spoils quicker than shitty food 'cause nothing good for you stays fresh for very long." He'd say, "The inside aisles at the supermarket are slow suicide."

At Publix we load the cart with ground chuck, refried beans, a can of Cheez Whiz, sour cream, taco spices, salsa, and guacamole. Mom grabs a case of Bud for herself and a two-liter bottle of Coke for me. She barrels down the aisle and says, "We need tortilla chips. It's an emergency."

We cook up everything, light vanilla-scented candles, crank Lady Gaga, and I dig into the tacos while Mom swills can after can of Bud and dabs her eyes. Her plate congeals into taco sculpture.

"Henry was right." She hurls an empty can over her shoulder. It bounces off the wall and lands in the overflowing laundry basket. "Put the wrong thing in your body and it poisons you." She picks up a fresh can, shakes it.

"It's gonna explode," I say.

She passes me the can. "You," she says.

I pop the tab and take a sip of the overflowing foam. My mouth tingles. I want to spit it out, but I swallow and say, "I like it."

She shrugs and holds up an invisible can. "To the future."

I tap the can against her knuckles and take another sip. Bubbles pop on my tongue and I wonder if the bitterness I taste means it's already skunked.

Touch That and the Doll Gets It

Rob's first-grade teacher, Mrs. Manning, sent all the parents an e-mail earlier in the week about some items that'd gone missing from the classroom. "We're not accusing any of the children," it read, "but we'd like parents to be aware that we most definitely have a thief in our midst. Please be sure to ask your child to take his or her personal items home at the end of the school day so we can avoid future thefts. And if any of the following items turn up at your house, please be sure to have your child return them to the rightful owner immediately."

The list includes:
- Mini flashlight
- Padlock
- Hair clip (pink)
- Barbie doll
- Dora the Explorer stickers

The naked Barbie lay on the table next to my water glass. When Rob brought Barbie home, still clothed in a powder blue flight attendant outfit, he didn't try to hide her. He'd gone so far as to bring her to the table and pull off her dress. Everything else, including an uninventoried, rhinestone-encrusted fake fingernail, had been piling up in his nightstand all week. I was waiting for the right moment to mention Mrs. Manning's e-mail. Surely she'd noted the timing of Rob's return and the missing items.

"Who's your friend?" I picked Barbie up and put her back down almost immediately. For a long time he didn't answer. We both sat listening to the occasional car pass the house.

The heater kicked on, and Rob said, "Is that what Mom looked like?" His index finger was buried knuckle-deep in his nostril. He looked at his plate and gave his finger a twist.

"Don't you remember?" I picked up my fork and knife and sawed into my cold steak. "Go wash your hands and then eat up."

Rob extracted his finger, without the audible pop I'd expected, and inspected his fingertip. He reached for a roll.

"Touch that and the doll gets it." I raised my knife above Barbie's torso. "Go," I said.

He shrugged, pushed away from the table, and zig-zagged down the hall to the bathroom. I heard the faucet turn on and off quickly. As he tromped back down the hall, flapping his hands, I looked for the limp that'd recently disappeared.

I put down my fork. "Let's see."

Rob extended his hands. I felt the dampness in his palms, nodded, and handed him a roll. He took a bite and sat down. "Not really," he said. "Well, kind of." He reached for the butter. "It's hot in here."

I'd recently taken to setting the thermostat at eighty. Any lower and I felt a chill. "Kind of what?"

"Kind of remember Mom. Can you do this?"

I buttered his roll and tried to ignore Barbie. Most of her body lay on the table surface, but her feet rested on my placemat, and this annoyed me the way it annoyed me when Joni used to slip off her shoes and toss her feet on the dashboard during the long weekend drives to the lake. I handed him back the roll and cut myself a wedge of steak that I ended up chewing like old gum.

"Her hair was darker. That's all I remember." Rob scratched his nose and wiped something on his leg.

"Slightly darker," I managed. "How about another roll? I can butter it. Just say the word."

I scooted back my placemat until Barbie's heels hit oak.

"I'm still finishing this one." He nibbled at the crust as if trying to prove his point. He chewed longer than it should've taken and stared at his plate. Finally he said, "When her hair got wet it got dark. Way darker than when it was dry. She filled the tub with bubbles and told me to sail my boat through the fog. We used to take baths together. She used different shampoo."

I wondered if Rob remembered the fog. The police said he'd floated to the surface face up and that the current deposited him on the shore with his legs still in the water—water so cold, the doctors said, that it could've killed him had he continued drifting. Weeks after the accident, he cried when they removed the casts, as if they were amputating his legs.

Later that night, after Rob was asleep, I rinsed the dishes, set the table for breakfast, took a long hot shower, and put out my clothes for the morning on the chest at the foot of the bed. For a while I tried to read but none of the words looked like words. My eyes kept passing over pages without absorbing a single sentence, so I turned off the light and curled up in a blanket like a cocoon and waited for my eyes to adjust to the dark. Outside the wind blew. Every once in a while a car passed and its headlights scanned the room. Each time another car approached, I closed my eyes before it passed, the headlights flashing across my lids. Then I kept my eyes closed until the sound faded. This game got tiresome, so I got up and, without turning on the light, fumbled across the room and switched on my computer. While it booted up I tiptoed into Rob's room and eased open his nightstand drawer. He lay flat on his stomach, snoring. I took special care not to disturb his other loot when I fished out Barbie. Back in my room I seated her against the monitor. I pulled up Mrs. Manning's message and hit reply.

"Dear Mrs. Manning," I typed. "Thank you for alerting me of the recent crime wave at McCarthy Elementary. To be perfectly honest, I resent the implication that one of the children is to blame. Have you recently hired a new custodian? Have you considered your colleagues? Elementary school teachers don't earn very much.

"Regardless of who the guilty party is, I appreciate the warning, and I'll be sure to urge Rob to keep his personal belongings with him at all times. You can't be too cautious these days."

I hit send and turned off the monitor. The room went black. I sat for a long time listening for another car, and when I finally heard one approaching I watched it pass, wondering who was driving, if there were passengers, where they were going. Long after the rattle of the loose muffler disappeared, I sat waiting for someone else to drive by. The heater turned on with a whoosh, the first blast of hot air giving me goose bumps, which I took as a sign to go to bed. We lived on a side street. There would be no more passing traffic. I picked up Barbie and said, "It's getting late." I considered putting her in my own nightstand drawer, but instead pulled her into my blanket cocoon and hugged her to my chest where it was warm.

Stealing Home

My father gave my mother a monthly allowance of $400. She was expected to buy groceries, fill the car with gas, and give me lunch money for school; there was always plenty left over for her to buy Cosmopolitan magazine or donate money to the collection at church every week. She kept the roll of $20 bills stuffed in a gold satin clutch wallet hidden underneath her panties in her top drawer. She thought that was the one place I would never look—she thought wrong. I'd peel off at least one bill a week to buy baseball cards from Alan, the old Italian guy who owned the convenience store around the corner from my house. Alan loved baseball. He was always listening to games on the radio; and he always let me sit and listen with him while I drank root beer.

The year was 1976. I was eight years old. Fred Lynn was the American League's MVP.

We'd moved to Miami from Salem, Massachusetts, a year before, and I missed going to Fenway Park with my father. Even though we got to attend Spring Training in March, Florida didn't have a baseball team, and I missed going to a *real* park, the smell of Fenway Franks, popcorn, peanuts and Cracker Jack, all the things the song promises. Even the scratchy organ music. It was the year Lynn, Yazstremski, and Rice stood in the outfield, Fisk squatted behind the plate, and Eckersley stretched on the mound. The Red Sox were on the downswing from a botched series. We'd moved just weeks before the series began.

I knew the slippery texture of the Topps wax wrapper, the stale taste of the cardboard bubble gum, the anticipation of shuffling the cards, searching for a rookie or a team picture. I had the entire set of cards neatly arranged in numerical order in shoeboxes on my closet shelf.

Cards weren't all I bought. I branched out and paid for ice cream and candy for the neighborhood kids: Snow cones for Tammy; toasted almond for Kenny; Pop Rocks for Alison; even cigarettes for Joey, the black-toothed teenager who, a week after we'd moved in, had stolen my Radio Flyer and painted it blue and then charged me $1 for a ride in it. After they found out where the money was coming from, they never said please or thank you.

Kenny came home with me one night so I could show him where I got the money, and we found my father sitting in a chair in my room. My 1975 American League Champions Red Sox pennant hung above his head. I had a pocketful of new cards to add to the cards that were now strewn on the bed. My empty shoeboxes were on the floor. My father's eyes were moist, his face flushed. He stared at the cards.

"Kenny," he said, "I think it's time you went home." Kenny didn't even look at me. He just nodded at my father and walked out of my room. I heard his quick footsteps scurry down the hall, and after the screen door slammed my father said, "How much for your cards?"

I shrugged. I didn't know what he meant.

He said, "You can pay your mother back." His voice was choked. "How much for your cards?" he repeated.

I started crying, but I stared at him defiantly. "I don't know."

He picked up my cards and carelessly stuffed them back into the shoeboxes. I wanted to tell him to be careful, to not bend the corners, to keep them in order, but I remained silent.

After wiping his eyes, he took out his wallet and handed me a fistful of 20s. "Here," he said. "Mom's over at Mary's. Put these in her wallet before she gets home."

He picked up the boxes and pressed them between his arm and torso and walked out of the room, closing the door behind him.

I crumpled up the bills in my little fist. And I remembered the cards in my pocket. I stopped crying. I dropped the bills. I pulled the cards out, gently, and arranged them in numerical order. Reggie Jackson, Mike Schmidt, George Brett, and Pete Rose. No Red Sox, but a respectable score. I placed them on the shelf in my closet, naked and exposed for anyone to see.

My parents' room was dark. I fumbled through my mother's dresser drawer, looking for the cool satin of her wallet. Before I forced the crumpled bills in to join the others, I grabbed a fresh, clean bill from the neatly rolled wad and put it in my pocket. I ran out of the house, down the street to Alan's. Kenny was there with all the kids from the neighborhood sitting on the curb, their bikes all in a row leaning on kickstands. The Yankees vs. the Red Sox crackled on the radio.

Alan leaned against the doorframe. He said, "Look who's back."

Everyone looked blankly at me, as if I were a stranger. "Come on," I said.

I held the bill up for them to see. They jumped up and cheered just as the announcer screamed, "Another home run for Jim Rice! The Sox take the lead!"

Twictions

She'd cried once. It was when he said, "Your eyelids never move when you're asleep. You're so still it's as if you don't have any dreams." Now he'd truly taken everything.

Kim broke into Phil's house and hid in the closet. While she waited for him to come home, she bent all his hangers into nooses.

Lance and Juree had a boring sex life. They said, "Let's try to save our marriage! Let's buy each other randy sex toys!" Juree got furry handcuffs. Lance bought an X-Box.

Bill practiced his golf swing at the high school practice field. One day he found a dirty pink sweat suit. He gave it to his son, Ty. Ty wore it and got beaten up on the bus.

Birdman

It's Saturday, which is both a blessing—no work, no plans—and a curse—no work, no plans. You can barely lift your coffee mug, let alone check your ex-girlfriend's Facebook profile. Two hours is nowhere near enough sleep.

You have the whole day to see whether she's updated her status from Single to In a Relationship. You can't handle new photos of her posing with people you don't recognize—wide-shouldered men with sculpted sideburns, thin women waving ringless fingers. You smell her baby powder and Noxema. If she burned the final bridge and set her profile to Private you'll drown yourself in the bathtub. So for the first time since the breakup—has it really been a month?—you postpone trolling for clues of your ex-girlfriend's post-you life, and instead check your e-mail. For the time being, you decide to leave the cyberspying to Homeland Security.

There's a message from an address you don't recognize, and if not for the Rundgren subject line ("Hello, It's Me") you'd mark it as SPAM and delete. "Me," it turns out, is a different ex-girlfriend, ex-girlfriend-three-girlfriends-ago. You haven't heard from her in eight years, this ex-girlfriend who put all her faith in an endearingly pathetic trinity comprised of you, palm readings, and daily horoscopes. Despite (or because of) her questionable belief system, you had every intention of marrying ex-girlfriend-three-girlfriends-ago . . . that is, until you met ex-girlfriend-two-girlfriends-ago on a flight from Boston to San Francisco. You never considered proposing to ex-girlfriend-two-girlfriends-ago.

You sip your coffee, lean forward and click open ex-girlfriend-three-girlfriends-ago's e-mail. It's been a long time—"Can you believe it's been EIGHT YEARS?"—and she has no idea if you're married, if you're living in California, if you're alive at all, but she Googled your name and found this address and took a shot. She says she dreamed about you last night, and, "don't freak," you were driving on Rt. 101 and smashed head-on into an eighteen-wheeler and "flew like Superman" through the windshield into the truck's grill. Killed instantly. Not at all like Superman, you think. She asks if you're okay, asks you to respond ASAP so she can finally go back to sleep. She signs it "L, Me" and adds "P.S.: My husband is one tough Greek and I don't love him . . . I'm not sure I ever did. I still live in San Francisco, fyi. BTW, Where are you hiding?"

This is an awesome distraction. You realize that despite the fact that you die in her dream, the you ex-girlfriend-three-girlfriends-ago is writing to, the you you were eight years ago, is alive and well. Okay, not alive and well. Immortal the way dead actors in old movies are immortal. You picture ex-girlfriend-three-girlfriends-ago curled in bed, immortalizing you via REM montage: There you are hiking around the Grand Canyon in mud-caked boots; ordering espresso in Mill Valley; jogging across the Golden Gate with headphones wrapped around your skull; collapsing like an accordion against an eighteen-wheeler's grill. You start humming a Kinks song. You figure dying in a Technicolor past is better than living in a black-and-white present.

This is way too much to process all at once. The e-mail rewound you eight years, so you fast-forward five years, to the immediate aftermath of the breakup with ex-girlfriend-two-girlfriends-ago, to when you whined insufferably to anyone unfortunate enough to lend a sympathetic ear—

friends and family, colleagues, people in the grocery check-out line, and, eventually, cloaked chat room strangers—about how her increasingly unshakable faith in God and Country, which you found both frightening and enviable, *forced* your exit. For her own good. To preserve your sanity. When relating the story, which became more animated and detail-drenched with each retelling, you neglected to mention how ex-girlfriend-two-girlfriends-ago's clear convictions challenged your soft-focus agnosticism and ironic pose so profoundly that for the first time you lost faith in your non-faith, saw the irony of your irony. You neglected to mention the sobbing jags, bleeding nails, apnea, bruxism (and attendant form-fitting mouth guard, which you still wear), mail-order porn, Super-Sizing it, Zoloft, untrimmed ear hair, and serious consideration of the views expressed on small-hour talk radio.

While that's all true, sure, okay, fine . . . you know in your heart that the real reason you never proposed to ex-girlfriend-two-girlfriends-ago, the real reason you started making public comparisons between her nonexistent cellulite and cottage cheese, is she was smarter, stronger and better-looking than you were or ever would be, and this scared the shit out of you, cowed you, made you look more closely at yourself than you ever had in your life. If this were the jungle, you'd be in the pot and she'd be stirring. You realized you were dim, doughy and average, and you projected your weaknesses onto those closest to you because—you dim, doughy, average idiot!—they were closest to you.

This is precisely the kind of soul-searching candor you're trying to avoid.

But the genie is out of the bottle, the blinds are wide fucking open. Be honest with yourself: Ex-girlfriend-two-girlfriends-ago formed the weekly Bible study group and joined the NRA as acts of counter-terrorism. You were not at all surprised that she married Sam, an organic apple farmer she'd met on Match, two months after you moved to Florida. She kept her maiden name.

You set the coffee mug on the desk, reach up and pat your head, feeling for bumps or blood. You laugh at yourself for the first time in . . . God, you have no idea, but it's been a *long time.*

You close your eyes, extend your arms out in front of you, imagine flying head-first through a windshield, only instead of smashing into the eighteen-wheeler's grill, you soar into the sky, soar west toward San Francisco, blue terrycloth bathrobe flapping like a cape. It's been a long time since you've traveled across the country, longer even than since the last time you laughed at yourself. The wind flattens what's left of your hair. You open your mouth, gulp air, and note the topography below: fishing boats bobbing atop the warm blue waves of the Gulf of Mexico, a funeral parade in New Orleans, the sagebrush-choked ranches of Texas, the trapped water lapping the Hoover Dam, the eroding sand pyramids of Death Valley, the countless neighborhoods both separated and connected by cracked highways and humming wires. Your head reels. It's breathtaking. You should get out more often.

You aim for the Golden Gate Bridge, the scene where eight years before, while driving in your Saturn, you broke up with ex-girlfriend-three-girlfriends-ago.

Flying through time and space makes you wonder if, like Superman, you can reverse the Earth's rotation, turn back the clock, rewind the film to correct mistakes before they happen. Forget bulletproof skin, forget telepathic chit chats with dolphins, forget invisibility. X-ray vision, flight, and time travel are the best superpowers. A bolt of neural lightning reminds you that, off-screen, Christopher Reeve obeyed the laws of gravity.

After nosediving into S.F. Bay, you surface and get your bearings; you crawl through the shifting currents toward Alcatraz. As you pull yourself ashore, body dripping, you cut your hands on the jagged rocks covered with seagull shit. You lie on your back and pant at the sky and consider a newfound respect for Aquaman. Across the Bay, sea lions bark at the tourists snapping their pictures. Goosebumps cover your arms.

You wash your hands in the stinging salt water, wring your bathrobe as dry as you can, snap it in the breeze for good measure, and hopscotch over to the main cell house. You join a tour group. As you stroll behind them down Broadway, you notice that no one else is wearing a dripping blue bathrobe and squishy slippers. They're all wearing yellow day-glo t-shirts and headphones. You duck into Robert Stroud's cell, expecting to find a toilet and bunk, a splattered easel, dented paint tubes and jars of brushes soaking in turpentine. Instead, you find your desk, chair and computer.

You pull the barred door shut, cinch your robe, collapse in the chair, and snap up your mug. Never in your life have you craved hot coffee more. The mug's empty and cold, so you smash it against the wall. You wonder where the tour group went and if anyone will ever visit your cell again, or if you're trapped here alone, unable to paint yourself as a bird that could squeeze between the bars and fly away.

This is precisely the kind of soul-searching candor

you're trying to avoid.

You squint at the computer monitor to reread ex-girlfriend-three-girlfriends-ago's message, with the vague hope that her words will offer you an escape plan. As you read, you realize that she is brave—much braver than you ever were, are presently, and, you fear, ever will be. You realize that the dream—the broken windshield, the eighteen-wheeler, your death—is a pretense. It is well-intentioned bullshit, a dream of a dream. You should know. The only sincerity in her message: L, Me; PS:; FYI; and BTW.

You cry for the first time in . . . God, you have no idea but it's been a *long time* . . . and this is . . . this is good. There's no other word for it. *Good.* This goodness makes you feel connected, plugged in. Electrified. You rub your eyes and blink deliberately.

The only way to preserve this moment is by documenting it. You start typing what you think will be a brief, ironic response to ex-girlfriend-three-girlfriends-ago's message, but each word peels away another layer of insulation, and soon you're detailing your dream of flying across the country, of crashing, of escaping. You admit to sincere feelings that flicker into existence and hover in the space between permanence and atrophy.

After you finish, you reread what you've written and are surprised that it's a pretty good letter, honest and true, etc., and so you decide to Bcc ex-girlfriend-two-girlfriends-ago and the ex-girlfriend whose Facebook page you'll visit soon enough. Hitting "send" feels right and necessary, because you want them to know that, fyi, someone's out there dreaming of them and that, in case no one's mentioned it lately, they're all very much alive.

Danny's Visions

Danny was twelve years old when he realized he was a prophet. It came to him in the form of a vision one Sunday afternoon in September, as he lay in the gravel beneath Mrs. Gabriel's tan Duster, loosening exhaust bolts with a wrench he'd stolen from his father's workbench. When he saw the tires of Josh's new Huffy whiz by, he closed his eyes, and foresaw—"foresaw" being a word he'd learned that morning in church when Pastor Dale used it during a sermon on biblical fulfillment of prophecy—Josh wiping out in a patch of sand as he turned the corner onto Evans Circle. Seconds later Danny opened his eyes and watched his vision unfold: Josh's tires skidded sideways, the Huffy leaned to the left, and Josh's knee skipped across the asphalt before his whole body and the bike spun and tumbled into a heap in the middle of the street, the whole incident haloed in a swirling cloud of dust. It reminded Danny of the summer, of July 4, when his family went to Good Harbor Beach, in Gloucester, and he watched his father skip flat stones across the waves, a feat Danny couldn't mimic no matter how many times he tried.

Danny laughed so hard he hit his head on the muffler. He crawled out and stood up, a rusty X smudging his forehead.

Josh sat rocking in the street, wailing and hugging his injured leg. Blood oozed out of his knee into his sock and shorts. His shirt was torn at the shoulder; his bike's front tire was spinning.

Danny said, "I knew you'd fall."

Josh's head hung over his knee, his mouth silently agape, a thread of drool coiling into the wound.

Danny walked past him and righted the Huffy. He got on, balanced his weight on one foot, and placed the other on the pedal and pretended he was kick-starting a motorcycle. The chain had fallen off and now sagged into the patch of sand. A length of it was wedged between the rear frame and axle, locking the back tire. One of the handgrips hung flaccidly. "I predict you won't be riding this home."

Josh grabbed his bike from Danny. As he limped away, the rear tire left a skid mark in the sand.

An hour later, Danny sat hiding behind his mother's azaleas and watched across the street as Mr. Sumner tethered Jake to the red cable that ran between two maple trees in his front yard. Danny remained hidden while Mr. Sumner piled into his car with Mrs. Sumner and Izzy, their son and Danny's friend, and drove away for their Sunday evening ice cream run. ("Sundaes on Sunday!" Izzy called it.) As soon as the sound of their car had faded, Danny crossed the street and began spraying Jake in the face with the Nair he'd snagged from his mother's bathroom. At first Jake lunged, his teeth gnashing at Danny, and Danny would hold his ground long enough to spray Jake in the face and then retreat until Jake choked himself on his leash. Jake snapped back, caught his breath, lunged even harder, crazed and straining on his hind legs, the taut line threatening to snap, giving Danny an open shot at Jake's face. Then Jake would dash back to the maple tree and Danny would chase him and repeat the dance. The simple choreography thrilled Danny to the point of terror, but every time he considered dropping the can and going home, he felt a deep shame that sent him leaping again toward Jake.

Mike, Josh's brother, walked up to the edge of the Sumners' lawn and said, "What in the fuck are you doing to Jake?"

Danny ran to a safe spot out of Jake's range and said, "You said a swear word. I'm telling."

Jake whimpered and trotted over to the base of one of the maple trees. He rubbed his nose on the ground and pawed his ears.

Danny stuck his tongue out at Mike.

Mike was 15, and wore a tight, sleeveless Iron Maiden t-shirt that displayed his round biceps that coiled purple beneath his thin white skin. Mike smoked Marlboros in front of his parents and was rumored to trim his fuzzy mustache with the hunting knife sheathed on his leather belt. Mike's father owned a barbershop in East Boston but a few months before Danny had overheard his mother and Mrs. Cronin say that the shop was just a front. Mike's father was really a bookie. "How else could they afford that house?" Mrs. Cronin had said to Danny's mother while they played gin and chain smoked at the kitchen table. Danny didn't know what a bookie was but he discovered it probably wasn't a good thing because when he asked Mike if his father sold books, Mike had punched him in the shoulder so many times that it took two weeks for the bruise to disappear. When Danny's father saw the bruise, he'd called Mike's father and told him if Mike ever laid a hand on Danny again, there'd be hell to pay. The next day Mike came by the house to apologize and gave Danny a cassette of Van Halen's *Fair Warning* as a peace offering. Danny had pulled out all the tape and used it to lash a dead garter snake to the Askers' mailbox.

Mike said, "You the one who laughed at Josh?" He crossed the lawn and towered before Danny.

Danny shook the Nair can and giggled at the memory of Josh's knee skipping across the asphalt.

Mike said, "He's with my mother at the hospital getting stitches." He snapped his neck back and forth, the way he had right before he'd pummeled Danny's shoulder.

"Hold it right there, partner," Danny said. He pointed the sprayer at Mike's face. "Or you're going to have a bad hair day."

Mike straightened his head and smirked. "I don't care who your daddy is," he said. "Think you'll be laughing when I stick that can up your ass?"

"More swears. I'm telling on you."

"You think I give a fuck, you fucking fuckity fucknut?"

When Danny laughed, Mike knocked the Nair out of his hand and wrestled him to the ground. Mike sat on Danny's chest, pinning his arms with his knees. From where he landed, Danny could turn his head and see Jake panting on his side in the shadow beneath the tree. Bubbles of saliva popped from Jake's mouth. Danny kicked but couldn't get free.

"Who's laughing now?" Mike leaned his full weight on Danny's arms.

Danny bucked and kicked, and Mike leaned in harder.

Mike reached over and grabbed the can of Nair next to Danny's open hand. He shook it and said, "Plenty left." He held the sprayer an inch from Danny's eye.

Danny squeezed his eyelids shut and had another vision. He foresaw himself flipping Mike off and reversing their positions—his knees pinning Mike's menacing biceps, his weight rendering Mike helpless, the Nair can steady in his hand and pointed an inch from Mike's eye. He could see it clearly, and the power of the vision sent his legs kicking, his hips bucking. But Mike was too heavy, his will and body too strong. After a full minute of fruitless effort, Danny went limp and opened his eyes. Mike was looking over at Jake as if he'd forgotten about Danny. Danny followed Mike's gaze. Jake's ribcage trembled, his shallow panting slowed to a wheeze. Mike turned back at Danny and said, "I know exactly what I'm doing. Let's see if we can wash that X off your forehead."

Danny closed his eyes and summoned all his holy power to fill Mike's heart with love and mercy and forgiveness. The first spray was cool, at first, almost refreshing after all the struggle. But as the sprays kept coming his skin began burning like hell's own fire and he surrendered all his pride and screamed for a father who wasn't there to save him.

Twictions

Whether he dies tomorrow or fifty years from now, he knows he'll be thinking of Monica. He doesn't want to die without her, but she's gone, so he joins a gym and exercises.

Kissee buys a parrot, names it Freud. When Freud repeats what she says, Kissee realizes that she's the reason all her relationships fail. She sets Freud free.

Ted knew Judy wouldn't grant him a divorce, so he pretended to love her more than when he'd really loved her. One day, he rented them a canoe and brought only one life vest.

Rick looked up from his book & asked his mom the difference between mitosis & meiosis. She said, "One's the way you were born and one's the way Jesus was born." Rick cried.

Evolution

When I was seven I asked my mother, "Why does dad call me his little field goal kicker?" She said, "When I was pregnant with you, your father was making love to me and you kicked him." I said, "I don't remember." She said, "He does." I said, "What's making love mean?" She said, "Someday you'll find out."

"Someday you'll find out what it means to work hard for your money only to watch someone piss it away." That's what my father said as he spanked me after he found out I dumped my new chemistry set into the sewer. I had been playing chemist in my driveway when I took out a fresh beaker and mixed all the chemicals to see what would happen. The solution changed colors, going from ink blue to dusk purple to black each time I added a new liquid. I used the red plastic eyedropper to stir it up and when I pulled it out the end had melted. A few drops fell to the asphalt and smoke began to rise. I covered my nose and mouth, afraid to inhale. My mother was pregnant at the time with my younger brother, and all I could imagine was her walking over the spilled chemicals and inhaling the fumes, infecting her fetus, causing a deformity or miscarriage. I scrubbed the area with Palmolive and hosed down the whole driveway. I put the chemistry set back in the box and ran down the street to the nearest sewer grate, poured each chemical into the sewer one by one, then smashed the tubes and beakers against the grate, the shards mixing with the tainted water. My hands were shaking.

My hands were shaking from the sugar rush. I'd drunk a whole six pack of Sprite from the case my father hid under the stairs in the cellar. I crushed the empty cans and buried them under some ashes in the bin behind the furnace.

Behind the furnace was a case of beer. Jason hoisted it on his shoulder and headed for the back door. I was in the kitchen drinking milk out of a carton. It was the third time in a month we'd robbed this house. (Why does this guy never lock his sliding glass door?) Matt came out of the bedroom with his hands behind his back and said, "Look what I found." He produced a sandwich bag stuffed with grass and a large manila envelope. I took one more swig of milk, dropped the carton on the floor, picked up a red, white, and blue campaign sign, and dashed for the door with Matt. Jason was looking around the corner of the house to make sure no cars were coming. We ran to the woods at the end of the street, climbed up into our tree fort, cracked open three beers, toasted our successful mission. I propped the sign in the corner on an old milk crate. Matt said, "Can you believe that guy's running for Mayor?" He shook the envelope until pictures of the guy whose house we'd just robbed littered the floor. Men and women—whole groups of them—performing acts you only heard about from older brothers and old men behind the supermarket. One of the pictures was of Mrs. O'Brien, my first-grade teacher. When I was six I had had a crush on her. I rolled her picture into a tight tube and slipped it into my empty beer can. All I could think was, pictures trap you.

Pictures trap you where you once were and act as evidence by showing what you've evolved into from a fixed point in time. That's why I bought a camera—so I could be on the safe side of the lens. On winter days Craig and I used to break into the icehouse near Crystal Lake Cemetery and check out the corpses waiting to be buried in the spring when the ground thawed. The bodies were stiff, ivory blue, naked, and cold, but you couldn't smell them; all you could smell was the stinging freshness of the cold. Craig stood next to a stack of bodies and I took the shot. Nobody's going to see where I've been, and nobody's going to gauge what I've evolved from.

I've evolved from a man in a boy's body into a boy in a man's body.

A man's body replaces itself every seven years. Old cells die and give birth to new. At fourteen I grew into my third body. How is it that the new body has the memories of the old? The scar I got at three when I chased a butterfly and fell off my father's loading dock, halfway through my first body, remains on my thigh. Wouldn't a new body recognize imperfections and correct them? If not, why the endless rebirth? By the power of suggestion, could I will my cells to give me bigger hands, smoother skin, smaller ears, a straighter nose, broader shoulders, longer legs, something, anything to correct my cells' perfect recollection of imperfection? Something to justify my genetic injustice?

"Justice will be served," said the football coach, "when we catch the little vandals who did this." According to the newspaper article, someone didn't like that the city had decided to cut down all the trees behind the 7-11 to pave a parking lot for the athletic field. Someone—and it must have been a group of someones because those cement sewer pipes are too heavy to be lifted by an individual—systema-tically dropped all the pipes on top of each other, cracking them into uselessness. Someone also took all the tires used during football practice, stacked them up on the goal post and lit them on fire, sending great black clouds into the air. That same someone—or someones, it is suspected—also found a way to bend the goal post to the ground, like a divining rod pointing to a hidden reservoir, after the firemen's hoses had extinguished the flames. The headline read: "What goes up must come down."

"Come down from there," my mother said. "This instant." I was on the roof stargazing, and by the position of the moon I knew it was past my bedtime, but I was waiting for the moon to disappear so I could see the stars more clearly. The moon is the stargazer's greatest enemy, next to mothers who won't let their sons be astronomers because there's school in the morning.

In the morning Michelle and I get dressed, sneak out of my room and out the back door. A few stars are visible in the morning sky. She tells me to pull over and park. I ask her which house is hers and she says it's around the corner. I hand her the rose I bought her the night before from the street vendor in Copley Square. She slips it inside her coat, pecks me on the lips, and runs around the corner. When I try to call her that night I find out she's given me a fake number. When I drive around her neighborhood I pass each house slowly, wondering which walls contain her, seeing if anyone's peeking out her front door at me.

If anyone's peeking out her front door at me, I can't see him, and this damn pizza's burning my hands. Kids always do this, order a pizza and disappear. Or else they send it to the house of some kid they're torturing that week, along with four other pizzas, five taxis, $90 worth of Chinese, a fire truck, and an ambulance. I sense the giggles laughing at me behind my back; I feel the eyes from a neighboring house watching me. I ring the bell and wait. I knock on the door and wait. I toss the pizza like a frisbee across the yard and the door opens. A middle-aged man wearing overalls says, "Sorry, I was in the bathroom."

In the bathroom; behind the cemetery; in the woods; on the ladder of the water tower; on the roof of the church; in the cars of the salvage yard; between the rocks at the beach; under the bridge by the train tracks; in the drainage pipe near the sub shop; on the island in the middle of Devil's Dishful pond; behind closed eyes—these are the places you go to be you.

You. You can never look me in the eye when we talk. If I were a woman I'd think you were checking out my chest, but I'm not and you're not. Flies can see you coming at them from any direction except directly above. What direction are you coming from?

What direction are you coming from? If you don't know yet, some day you'll find out. When we circled each other seeing who would throw the first punch, swearing, my hands were shaking. Whole systems of ice tunnels beneath the wet snow in my yard, and when it was time to come in I'd warm myself behind the furnace. Not a single photograph exists of me after the age of fourteen. If I disappeared today those old pictures would trap me at that age. Darwinists still can't account for the missing link, so I still wonder what cast molded me and what I've evolved from. A man's body betrays years of punishment. If we each lived life alone would we still grow, or is it changing conditions and people that mold us? Eva never knew I loved her. If I'd had the courage to speak, we'd have disappeared into the woods. The front door closed for me a long time ago, but I still sneak in the back and watch the slideshow from the shadows. Sometimes I hold my breath in the bathroom as you pass by. One day at school, when I was thirteen years old, Rosemary and I snuck into a small patch of trees and bushes behind the rectory garage. There, behind a camouflage of rhododendrons and maple leaves, I found out what it was to make love.

Ruby, My Dear

Amy had just packed her bags and moved out that morning. I was sitting in my living room, drinking gin. There was a knock at my door. I looked through the peephole. Ruby sat in her wheelchair, her gray hair pulled back in a tight ponytail, her remaining leg pointing at the door.

"Bill's gone, Gabe," she said to the door.

"So's Amy." I clinked the ice in my glass.

"C'mon," she said, and turned her wheelchair around.

I opened the door and followed her down the hall. "When?"

"Five minutes ago," she called over her shoulder.

We went into her apartment. The windows were all open, a hot breeze blowing through the curtains. I closed the door behind me.

"Want me to call someone?"

"I need you to help me bury him."

"The funeral home?"

"I mean *bury* Bill," she said slowly. "In the Everglades."

I looked around her apartment. There were two old sofas facing a television, a coffee table covered in glasses with straws sticking out of their mouths. The rug had wheel imprints zig-zagging in every direction. Above the entertainment center was a black and white photo of Ruby and Bill dancing at their wedding.

Ruby said, "It's what he wanted."

"Isn't that illegal?" Gin and thoughts of Amy floated through my head. I was trying to wrap my brain around what Ruby was saying.

"My husband's dead." She wheeled right up to me, her remaining leg bumping into my knee.

I stepped back. What about death certificates and calls to the coroner and police? Was there some Everglades Cemetery I hadn't heard of?

Ruby said, "Tonight, after we go to the Everglades, you'll drive me to the beach and wheel me down to the water's edge. I'm going to say that Bill and I were down there and that he wanted to feel the water. He lowered himself out of the chair and a big wave came and took him away. My wheels got stuck in the sand and I couldn't help him."

Direction. A concrete plan. Now I could see what Ruby was getting at. I didn't like it. I wanted to run back to my apartment, pour another glass of gin, turn up my music, and forget about Ruby and Bill, wallow in my misery over Amy. Instead, I said, "This won't work. They'll search the beach and the water. They'll ask how you got down there in the first place."

"I'll say you dropped us off. I'll say you've been doing that for us once a week. You don't have to stick around. Just leave me and Bill's chair there and once I know you're gone and no one saw us I'll start screaming my head off for help. Who's going to doubt an old lady in a wheelchair?" She really *had* thought this through.

I walked to the kitchen and picked up the phone.

"Put down the phone," she said. "You promised to help me. Bill's in the bedroom. If I weren't in this damn wheelchair I'd do it myself, but I am and I can't."

Her steady voice, her resolve, surprised me. Didn't she want to give her husband a proper burial? Wasn't she going to cry? If Amy and I had stayed together for the next fifty years, would she ditch my body in a swamp if I asked her? Doubtful. Amy wouldn't even go to a ball game or a Thai restaurant with me. But Amy wasn't Ruby and I wasn't Bill. Ruby had had years to prepare for this. Maybe this was a proper burial in her eyes. She looked up at me and nodded.

We waited until dark. After we zipped Bill up inside a sleeping bag, Ruby took the elevator down to make sure no one was around. I looked out the window to the parking lot. She was there by my car, sitting under the moth-infested streetlight, waving for me to come down, her pocketbook in her lap. I nearly called the police. My head was clear by that point and Ruby's plan seemed even more ludicrous than when I was tipsy. But, I supposed, a promise was a promise, and Ruby was old. And was she really asking so much of me? Aside from dragging a dead body, what was a ride to the Everglades? She'd spent a lifetime with Bill and this was what they'd decided. Who was I to spoil their plans? I couldn't even keep a girlfriend let alone sustain a marriage, so maybe love meant burying your husband in a swamp. I picked Bill up and headed downstairs.

When I placed Bill in the trunk of my old Cadillac, the shocks absorbed him as they would a pothole. He would have been heavier, and far less manageable, had he not lost his legs to diabetes. I ran back upstairs, grabbed his folded-up wheelchair, raced downstairs, and tossed it in the trunk next to him. I closed the trunk and squatted down by the side of the car, panting.

"You've got the stamina of a rock. No wonder Amy left," Ruby said. She caressed the handle of her wheelchair.

We sat still for a few moments, the buzzing of the light and bugs above us. "We should probably go now," I said.

She wheeled up to the passenger door. "Help me in, if you can manage."

I unlocked the door, picked her up under the leg and back, noticed how light she was compared to Bill, and put her down gently in the front seat. I folded up her chair and put it in the back seat, then got in and started the car.

We turned onto Route 95 north, heading toward Ft. Lauderdale. Ruby struck a wooden match on the dashboard, lit a cigarette and coughed. "You mind?" she said, cracking the window. The smoke swirled out with the wind. "Don't ever smoke," she said as she exhaled. "Too late for me. My water's already polluted."

"Can I ask you something?"

"Shoot."

"Is this really the way Bill wanted it? You don't have to answer. But you have to admit this is—"

"Odd?"

"Fucked."

She took a drag of her cigarette and squinted. "It was what we decided. If I went first, then you'd be talking to Bill and I'd be in the trunk."

"Why not the ocean? Seems more dignified than the Everglades."

"This has nothing to do with dignity." She inhaled deeply on the cigarette. "He'd be washed up by the tide. They'll never find him in the Everglades. We discussed the options."

She flicked her cigarette out the window. I looked in the rearview mirror, saw a flurry of red ash skittering across the dark asphalt.

"Please, use the ashtray."

"You an environmentalist?"

"I just don't feel like getting pulled over for littering."
She laughed.

I turned on the radio and scanned through the stations. We passed a sign that read: Route 75 Alligator Alley. My headlights sliced through the darkness. We drove the rest of the way without talking, listening to the radio.

As we drove I thought about Amy. I thought about how she'd been in such a rush to leave that on her way to the door she banged her knee on the coffee table and didn't even flinch. I thought about what she said to me—that I was too detached, too self-absorbed, that I was too apathetic about work, our relationship, "life in general." She was right, of course, but I can't imagine that she just woke up one day, looked at me and thought that I should have more passion about being a pizza chef. She knew from the start that I wasn't and probably never would be a career man. No surprises there. No, her vague list of excuses was really a scapegoat for the real problem—my insisting she get an abortion last year, a decision that we reached together after a short discussion over breakfast. Ever since we drove up to the clinic and walked past the picket line of protestors, Amy hasn't seen me as anything but an accomplice to murder. I wondered what she'd think of my driving toward the Everglades with Bill in my trunk.

Ruby pointed to a stretch of dirt on the side of the highway in the distance. "Pull over."

I cut the engine and turned off the lights. Millions of bugs chattered around us like humming wires. A small hill led down from the turnaround to a canal that ran parallel to the highway. A chain link fence stood between the water and us.

"You'll be quicker without me." She lit another cigarette and stared straight ahead.

I sighed and got out. No headlights were coming from either direction. I hauled the sleeping bag out of the trunk and laid it by the side of the car. After slamming the trunk shut I walked around to Ruby's window and knocked. "Where should I bring him?"

She spoke through the small opening in the window, "Bring him in as far as you can and make sure he's under water."

"There's a fence." I pointed to the bottom of the hill where the chain link fence extended as far as I could see in either direction. "And there's alligators around here—now— probably listening to this conversation."

"Bill liked himself a good fried alligator with hot sauce."

Great, they'll have their revenge. I nearly picked Bill up, put him back in the trunk and drove home. I thought if I saw a cop along the way I'd beep and tell him I had a dead body in the trunk and did he know where I could drop it off. Instead I just stood there listening to the bugs, thinking I should call Amy.

"Please, Gabe," said Ruby. Her voice cracked, as if embarrassed by this whole thing herself, as if she'd rather have given Bill a traditional funeral, that she would rather be anywhere else but here, and would I please just hurry up and get this whole thing over with because she and I were partners and we'd both promised Bill to take care of things when he was gone. I thought of the way Amy used to say, "Please, Gabe," when we argued. Ruby shook the box of wooden matches like a baby shaking a rattle.

"What if he doesn't sink?"

"The sleeping bag is old and made of cotton. Very absorbent."

"Do you want to say goodbye?"

"We already did." She shook the matchbox again.

"Beep if you see any headlights," I said. I picked up Bill and staggered with him down the hill, trying not to lose my footing, trying not to slip into the fence. I hoisted it—him—above my head and onto the top of the fence. The sleeping bag got momentarily stuck on one of the spikes, ripped free, then fell over to the other side. It rolled into the canal, bobbed, spun like a log and sank the way you see in movies. I stood there for a minute to make sure he didn't pop back up. The only thing that rose to the surface was a few bubbles. Ruby beeped. I scrambled up the hill pretending to zip my fly. A car whizzed past, kicking up a backdraft of gravel into my face.

I turned on the radio and began flipping through the stations again. "Stop there," said Ruby, touching my hand. It was a somber solo jazz piano piece, a ballad. Ruby closed her eyes. I pulled onto Route 95, south to Hollywood. The song ended and the station went to commercial. Ruby opened her eyes and said, "Change the station." She lit another cigarette.

I turned the radio off.

She exhaled and said, "I thought for a minute that it was 'Ruby, My Dear,' but it wasn't. Wishful thinking. Bill and I used to go see Thelonious Monk in New York in the 50's and 60's, and whenever he played 'Ruby, My Dear' Bill would squeeze my knee under the cocktail table and lean over to kiss me." She paused. "Didn't you say Amy was gone?"

"Left this morning."

"I'm sorry."

"You're sorry? I'm sorry, Ruby. Bill *died*. Amy just left."

"How long were you together?"

"A little over a year. You and Bill?"

"Fifty-three."

I wanted to get home to call Amy and tell her about this. There was no way to turn back the clock or bring the baby back, but maybe we could start over fresh. "Ruby, can I ask you something? I know you're mourning and all, so you might not want to discuss anything, but how did you and Bill make things work?"

She stared through the windshield for a while before answering. "All I can say is that we had to keep falling back into love all the time, which means we kept falling back into hate or apathy or disgust all the time, too. There's bliss, there's joy, there's passion, sure, but there's also the most god-awful cruelty. Love fills you and kills you at the same time." She paused for a moment and then said, "I think commitment is important. And respect. Shared values. All that. But the core is tolerance. You have to tolerate each other, 'cause God knows we're all pains in the ass. If we can't tolerate each other's failings, we all might as well feed ourselves to the alligators. A year? Sometimes a year's as much time as you need. Sometimes," she said, "if it's good, if it's real good, a year is a lifetime."

I sped up as we approached the exit. I rolled down my window, filled my lungs with fresh air. I could smell the saltiness of the ocean. Ruby kept talking: "Bill used to play that song for me on the piano. God, he was awful."

All I wanted to do was get home, call Amy. If we patch things up, I'll tell her all about this. But first I had to drop Ruby at the beach.

Acknowledgments

Thanks to all the editors who originally published these stories.

Thanks to my friends, students and colleagues at Florida Gulf Coast University, including but not limited to: Kevin Aho, Jill Allen, Kevin Allen, Carol Bledsoe, Sheila Bolduc-Simpson, Jim Brock, Lori Cornelius, Allison Dieppa, Jason Elek, Robert Gregerson, Conan Griffin, Julie Griffin, Jim Gustafson, Kimberly Jackson, Erica Krueger, Myra Mendible, Eric Otto, Linda Rowland, Paul Szczesny, Rebecca Totaro, Joe Wisdom, and the whole Language & Literature gang. I'm incredibly lucky to work with such smart, supportive people.

The seeds for some of these stories were written in the basement of a strip mall in Peabody, MA, during my breaks as a line cook at Mr. G's Pizza. Thanks to Kat and Mark DeLomba for the work, the food, and the room with no view.

Every writer should be so lucky to receive a residency at the Fundación Valparaíso in Mojacar, Spain. Thanks to Pilar Parra and her staff, I was given the time and space to spend four glorious weeks staring out the window at the Mediterranean, sipping tea and sangria, and filling legal pads with my scribbles.

Much love to The Circle for their support and countless potluck dinners: Karyn Everham, Win Everham, Christopher Michaels, Jesse Millner, Lyn Millner, Maria Roca, Martha Rosenthal, Jim Wohlpart, and Sasha Wohlpart.

I'm deeply grateful to the many talented authors, editors, teachers and friends who influenced the writing of these stories through their direct advice and/or artistic example: Erin Almond, Jonathan Ames, MK Asante, Andrea Askowitz, Julianna Baggott, Dan Bern, Craig Bernthal, Richard Blanco, Charles Bock, John Bond, John Brandon, Augusten Burroughs, Robert Olen Butler, Bonnie Jo Campbell, Kevin Canty, Christopher Castellani, Cindy Chinelly, Steven Church, Brock Clarke, Sloane Crosley, Eugene Cross, Ron Currie Jr., John Darnielle, Denise Duhamel, Craig Finn, Nick Flynn, Gina Frangello, Emily Franklin, Tom

Franklin, Roxane Gay, Billy Giraldi, Stephanie Elizondo Griest, Chuck Hanzlicek, Nate Hill, Alice Hoffmann, Kristen Iversen, Leslie Jamison, Walter Kirn, Steve Kistulentz, Christina Baker Kline, Alex Lytton, Ron MacLean, Joyce Maynard, Campbell McGrath, John McNally, Joe Meno, Kate Miles, Dito Montiel, Dinty Moore, Keith Lee Morris, Tim O'Brien, Susan Orlean, Jeff Parker, Tim Parrish, Tom Piazza, Liz Prato, Chuck Radke, Rob Roberge, Henry Rollins, Richard Russo, John K. Samson, Julia Scheeres, David Sendler, Jim Shepard, Karen Shepard, George Singleton, Christine Sneed, Wesley Stace, Les Standiford, Michael Steinberg, Johnny Temple, Emma Trelles, Willy Vlautin, Jay Wexler, Robert Wilder, Liza Wieland, Tom Williams, Steve Yarbrough, and all of the fine writers who've presented at the Sanibel Island Writers Conference.

Thanks to my agent, Christopher Schelling, for his humor, intelligence, guidance, and keen contractual knowledge.

My great pals have given me so much encouragement and—perhaps unwittingly—material: Nicole Adams, Bailey Buchanan, Peter "Blaze" Corcoran, Ron and Mary Desisto, Mark Gentley, Richard Middleton-Kaplan, Craig Montoya, Michael Runnels, Britta and Marc Schulze, Craig and Stephanie ("Still working on that book?") Smith, and Jenn Toler.

Special thanks to Kevin Toler, my oldest friend, who designed this book's cover, and to Lynne Barrett and John Dufresne, for encouraging me in so many ways over the past two decades.

My father, William DeMarchi, a retired accountant, and my mother, Kathleen DeMarchi, a retired nurse, are the most practical people I know, yet they never once made me feel foolish for chasing imaginary people around on a page. Extra special thanks to them and to the rest of my family for being such staunch cheerleaders: Andrea DeMarchi, Michael DeMarchi, Tiffany DeMarchi, Jonny Markowitz, Ruthie Wenger, Karen Tolchin, and Martin Tolchin.

To my son, Charlie Tolchin DeMarchi: This book is for you.